This Little Tiger book belongs to:

_____

_____

_____

LITTLE TIGER PRESS LTD,
an imprint of the Little Tiger Group
1 Coda Studios, 189 Munster Road, London SW6 6AW
www.littletiger.co.uk

First published in Great Britain 2015
This edition published 2015

Text copyright © Steve Smallman 2015
Illustrations copyright © Ada Grey 2015
Steve Smallman and Ada Grey have asserted their
rights to be identified as the author and
illustrator of this work under the Copyright,
Designs and Patents Act, 1988

A CIP catalogue record for this book is available from
the British Library

Printed in China
LTP/2700/3191/0220
10 9 8

For Gabriella, who makes the BEST animal noises EVER! – S S

To GavGav, POOP, PARP, PHWEEP! – A G

Hippobottymus

written by
STEVE SMALLMAN

illustrated by **ADA GREY**

LITTLE TIGER
LONDON

A mouse sat down by a bubbling creek –
The creek went **bubble** and
the mouse went squeak!

Squeak, squeak, bubble, bubble,
squeak, squeak, squeak.
Squeak, squeak,
bubble, bubble,
squeak, squeak,
squeak!

A little bird tweeted,

"What a
GREAT song!

And if you don't mind,
I'll sing along!"

"Wait!" yelled Centipede. "You need a beat!" So he tapped out a rhythm with his tappity feet...

Tip-tap-a-tippy-tappy, tweet-tweet-tweet,

Squeak, squeak, bubble, bubble, squeak, Squeak, **Squeak!**

Monkey heard the music and he cried, "**Woo-hoo!** That sounds so **cool**, can I join in too?"

Warthog said,
"I'VE GOT A MUSICAL BUM!"
Then he banged on his bottom like a big bass drum...

odile.

He listened to the music
and it made him smile!
He reached in his pocket
and he took out a bone...

...Then he played on his teeth like a xylophone!

PLINK PLINK PLINK-A-PLONK!
PLINKETTY-PLOO!

BOOM-BA-DA-BOOM-BOOM!

Ooh, ooh, ooh!

Tip-tap-a-tippy-tappy,
tweet-tweet-tweet.
Squeak, squeak, bubble, bubble,
squeak, squeak,
squeak!

Well they danced and they played till a quarter to four,
Then they all flopped down in a heap on the floor.
"Wow!" cheered Mouse. "Now, wasn't that fun?
You guys ROCKED! Hooray! Well done!"

"Thanks!" they cried. "We helped, it's true,
But the person we should
thank is..."

"Excuse me?" Mouse said. "But what did you do?
Monkey was the one who went ooh, ooh, ooh!
Centipede **tapped** with his **tappity** feet,
And this little bird went tweet, tweet, tweet."

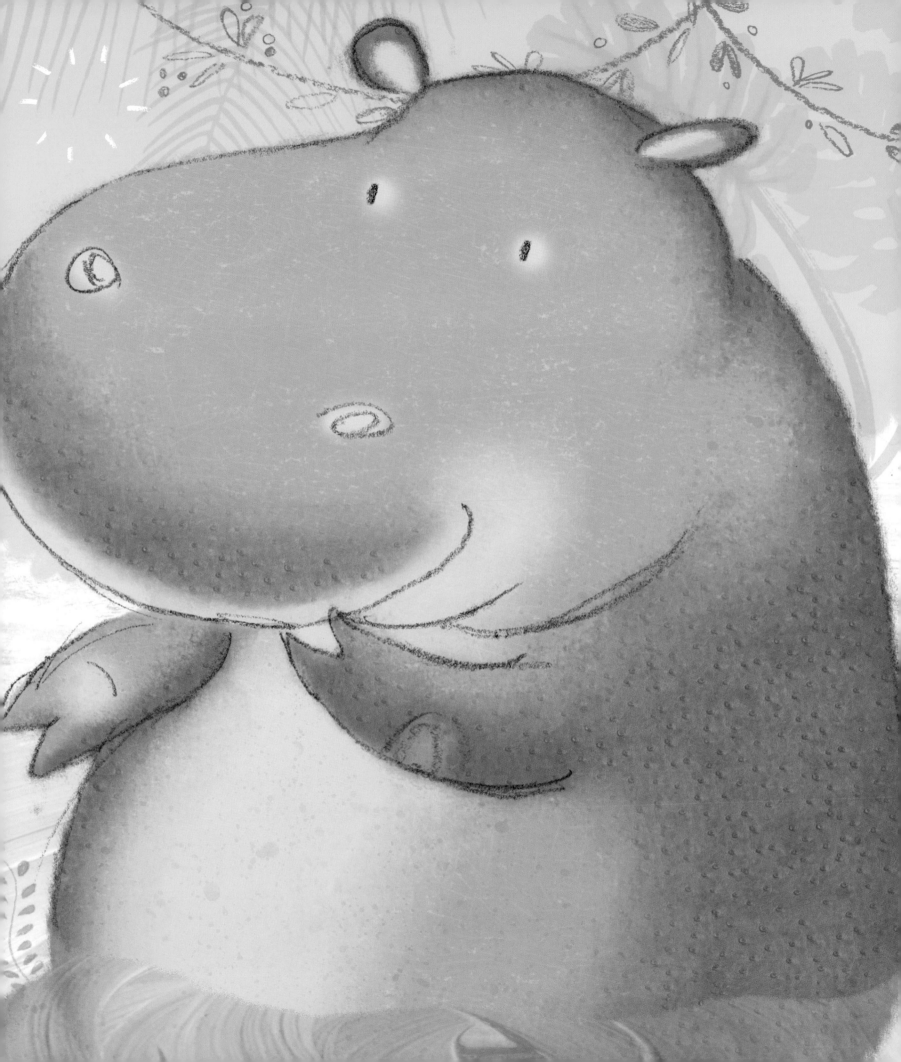

"Warthog banged on his musical bum –
It went BOOM-BA-DA-BOOM!
like a big bass drum!
Crocodile played plink, plinketty-ploo,

And I went squeak so...
WHAT DID YOU DO?"

Hippo said,
"Well, I ate beans this week...
My bottom made the **bubbles**
in the **bubbling** creek!"

TRUMP-PARP-bubble-bubble!

TRUMP-PARP-POP!

"My botty's blowing bubbles and it just won't stop!"